The Savannah House

Jamie O'Connor

First Edition Trade Paperback

Copyright © 2014 Chloe Garner

Published by A Horse Called Alpha

ISBN-13:   978-0615960654
ISBN-10:   0615960650

For all the people who smiled
when I told them I wanted to be a writer.

The most important thing in Gennie's life was food, until it was Ari.

The day after high school graduation, she had packed up her beat-up Subaru and driven from her home in the deep south of Georgia to a cooking school in New York City. Center of the food world, she thought. No place she'd rather be. A love of eating doesn't confer an inevitable culinary capability, though, and she quickly found herself in the middle of the pack within her class, struggling to tread water for her own dishes, but highly sought after as a sous-chef. Her heart broke when she finally admitted to herself that her attention to detail and militaristic execution of instruction had led to a lack of creativity that was going to keep her from that prized title: head chef.

Ari, on the other hand, was a star. His kitchen was a one-man bazaar of pots, pans, and flying food accompanied by the strangest and most wonderful stories. His Japanese upbringing, television chefs he had seen, even stories he had heard about food from around the world, woven into a deft preparatory spectacle that it seemed only Gennie could keep up with. They were a match, much as she might have wished otherwise, and paired more and more frequently as their graduation drew nearer. How could she not have been dazzled by his wit and his talent? How could she ignore the obvious honor of being noticed and pursued by this up-and-coming, small-g-god of her chosen universe? The pain of a lost dream flitted away nearly un-noticed as Ari landed a small role on a network morning show and took her with him as the silent pair of hands that kept everything spinning. How could she complain? She was on television – *television* – with the man who had supplanted food as her first waking thought. Her southern belle's soft curves melted away as she ate less and worked harder, in everything being more like him. This was definitely what accomplishment looked like.

And now they were going home. To her home. She knew Ari's parents well – a severe, mostly-traditional Japanese couple who approved of her work ethic and her devotion, but who ever so quietly disapproved of her skin tone – but that was still in New York City. She could smile and nod and they would get through the evening, and then they would go *home*. Two tiny apartments of the same floor – they were both still a bit traditional, after all – where he would kiss her on the forehead goodnight and she would go to sleep with the sun still up, dreading with perverse anticipation the wicked slam of the alarm clock in the tiny hours of the next morning. Ari would be up, showered, clothed, and packed for the day by the time she stumbled over to his apartment for a quick breakfast. Normal.

Now they were going to *her* home. How different the word could be, prefaced like that. Leaving New York's swift efficiency and going to Savannah. To late mornings, heavy, fatty food, and her mother and sister leaning over her shoulder like a brace of doves, watching every move she made. She smiled nervously at Ari as they walked off the plane and he winked at her, squeezing her hand as he shifted the carry-on across his back. He wouldn't let her carry luggage. Her Ari wouldn't hear of it. She looked down at the long, slender fingers the color of unbleached flour closed around her hand and closed her eyes as they walked.

Past the security lines, Gennie picked out the pair of familiar faces.

"Genevieve!" her mother called, waving. Ari stepped up his pace.

"Hi, Momma," Gennie said. There it was. The drawl that she had worked for years to overcome, the one that she had had to tame just to get out of doing Southern cooking her whole life, back in the very first word out of her mouth to her mother. She had never had a chance.

Her mother pulled her inescapably into a long hug, then pushed her away with brisk finality.

"Well," the woman said.

"Ari, this is my momma, Suzanne, and my sister Carolyn," Gennie said. Ari's face told her that he had noticed the change in her dialect and was amused by it, but only in his usual, dry fashion.

"Ladies, I'm so glad to finally meet you," he said quickly, putting out his hand to Gennie's mother, shaking her hand, then turning to her sister.

"Lynn," Carolyn said, widening her eyes un-subtly at Gennie before she took Ari's hand.

"Since when?" Gennie asked.

"You've been gone a long time," Carolyn said, tilting her head saucily. Gennie subconsciously ticked off the incorrect diphthongs in the sentence as she rolled her eyes at her sister.

"Your sister has an important job, Lynn. We understand why she can't ever come home for holidays," her mother interrupted before Gennie could answer. Gennie closed her eyes.

"Momma," she started.

"C'mon, Sugar, let's go get your bags," her mother countered, taking Lynn's arm and turning away. "Then we can get all to know your new beau."

Ari pressed his lips with genuine humor and took Gennie's hand, wrapping it around his forearm.

They stood waiting for the baggage carousel to start running as Gennie's mother gossiped absent-mindedly with Lynn.

"Y'all're lucky to get here on such a pretty day," Suzanne said abruptly. "Not too hot yet."

"I think it's raining in New York," Ari answered.

"Does that a lot, does it?" Lynn asked.

"Enough," Ari answered.

"I can't imagine not bein' able to see the sky," Lynn said. Gennie sighed.

"We have sky in New York," she answered.

3

"Not as much, I bet," Lynn said, leaning forward to make another face about Ari around Suzanne. Gennie might have blushed, but the conveyor finally started running again. Ari, chivalrously not noticing Lynn, stepped forward to wait for the bag.

"You never said he was so hot," Lynn whispered.

"I sent you the links to our show online," Gennie said. Lynn shrugged.

"Still."

Ari swung the bag off the conveyor and turned back.

"Only one bag?" Suzanne asked meaningfully.

"Momma," Gennie warned.

"Cheaper only to check one," Ari said. "My stuff is separate."

Suzanne nodded skeptically.

"Where's Daddy?" Gennie asked, looking for another topic.

"Went ahead to play a round of golf with a client," Lynn answered, just as uncomfortable.

Again, Gennie regretted agreeing to drive down to Savannah with her mom.

"If it's about the money, just drive down with us. You can get a direct flight from New York to Atlanta, surely," her mother had said. Ari had interceded on behalf of not sitting at a terminal at the Atlanta airport for as long as it would have taken to drive the rest of the way, and the $200 savings per ticket didn't hurt, so she had gone along with it. How difficult could it be?

Now that it was here, though, four and a half hours in a car with the two of them made her feel sick. She loved her sister, and her momma even more, but she hadn't been caged in with the both of them in nearly eight years. She could always hang up the phone when she hit her limit, from New York.

"He said he'd be back in time for supper," Suzanne said, signaling that she was ready to head out by hefting her purse higher on her shoulder.

"He had better be," Ari said. "He's not going to want to miss it."

Lynn giggled.

"You're cookin' for us?" she asked.

"Of course he's cookin' for us, Darlin; that's what he does, and he's gonna wanna impress your Daddy," Suzanne said.

"Hadn't even crossed my mind," Ari said confidentially to Lynn. "I've just got some ideas I want to try out with a real Southern family."

Gennie had no doubt that he did. She smiled at the idea of him working in their Savannah kitchen, giving the gourmet appliances the workout they were designed for.

"What's on the menu?" Lynn asked. Ari winked.

"Secret," he said, holding up slightly to catch Gennie's hand. Lynn wrinkled her nose with a conspiratorial grin and jogged to catch up to Suzanne.

"Going great," Ari said softly into Gennie's ear, a smile in his voice. "They're very charming."

"I'm glad you're charmed," Gennie said, a bit of her New York edge returning to her voice. He laughed into her hair and momentarily pressed his cheekbone against her temple, then straightened, following Suzanne through the airport lobby and out into the parking garage.

Gennie and Ari had eaten in New York before they left, but Suzanne's first stop was drive through on the way out of the city for herself and Lynn.

"You two want Cokes?" she asked the back seat as the electronic voice on the speaker waited.

"I'd appreciate a water," Ari said.

"Coke," Gennie answered for herself. Suzanne turned harder in her seat.

"You sure?" she asked Ari.

"He doesn't drink much Coke, Momma," Gennie answered. Suzanne's eyebrows went up.

"Oh." It was one of those Momma words that said too much.

"Momma," Gennie sighed.

"Oh, if we did get a chance, though, I would like to stop and pick up a couple bottles of wine to go with dinner later this week," Ari said, as though just thinking of it. Gennie smiled out the window.

"Daddy doesn't drink wine," Lynn said. "How did you two meet?"

"Gennie was the one that everyone wanted to get to help them on projects," Ari answered. "I won out."

"You were popular?" Lynn asked. Gennie stuttered.

"Of course," Ari said. "She isn't popular here?"

"I'm a bit quiet for these parts," Gennie answered, slouching a bit. Lynn laughed.

"She couldn't carry a conversation with two people to hold up the ends for her," she said, taking her food from Suzanne. "Bless her heart."

Ari laughed.

"I haven't found that to be true at all."

"So did you hear that the Logan girl graduated med school?" Suzanne asked, handing back the drinks.

"She's got a little boy, now, too," Lynn added. "Her husband's a businessman in Macon."

"Gennie and the Logan girl," Suzanne said. 'Elisabeth,' Gennie supplied, "they graduated together."

"Were you friends?" Ari asked.

"The Logans are old family friends," Suzanne said. Gennie shrugged, sliding down further so that her momma couldn't see her, and grimaced at Ari.

"She was the prettiest girl on the island, every summer," Lynn said. Gennie nodded. That was certainly true.

"And Greta moved out," Suzanne said, signaling to merge onto the interstate.

"Where'd she go, again?" Lynn asked.

"Orlando," Suzanne said. "She's got family down that way."

"That house was too big for her to take care of all by herself, after Gregory died, anyway," Lynn said. Suzanne 'Mmm-hmm'ed her emphatic agreement. They had been Mr. and Mrs. Jackson to her, all those years ago, Gennie thought. When had they become Greta and Gregory?

"D'ja hear Stephen got married?" Suzanne asked, looking over her shoulder at Gennie. Gennie shrugged helplessly.

"Pretty lady from up north, here for school," Suzanne said.

"Yankee," Lynn commented.

"Hush," Suzanne replied, not unkindly.

"David's still single, Gennie," Suzanne said, sitting up so that she could see Gennie in the rearview.

"Momma," Gennie said, shrinking a bit further.

"David's her ex," Lynn supplied to Ari. Ari smiled.

"What does he do?" he asked.

"Construction for his daddy," Lynn said. "I hear he's still trying to get published."

Gennie closed her eyes, listening to her own breath. Then came the question she had known that this trip was for.

"So, Ari, tell us about yourself."

They pulled into the driveway of the house and Gennie sensed rather than heard Ari's breath stop.

"I should have warned you better," she whispered. She hadn't known how to explain it, and hadn't wanted to admit her claim to it, more significantly.

The Savannah house was a summer house that they had moved into every year after finals and left only days before the resumption of the school year each year. Her daddy had developed a client pool on the coast and had leveraged a spot in the community into a serious stream of income. Gennie didn't know exactly how much income, and she didn't want to know.

The house was at least six-thousand square feet on most of five acres of river-front land with an outdoor kitchen, a pool, a hot tub, and a gazebo out back, and a long, sprawling driveway out front.

Driving up to the house, Gennie knew that her two lives were ashamed of each other, but she was less certain for a moment which of them was her real life. Ari whistled.

"We're going to need more wine," he said.

"You should see what we've got before you go out and buy more," Suzanne said. "The kitchen is supposed to be stocked, but I always have to go shopping, anyway, because they never do it right."

"I'll make a list," Ari said, still staring at the house. "Do you have a farmer's market?"

"Every day," Suzanne said, "but we missed it, today, Hon. They'll 'a mostly packed up by 5 or so."

Ari smiled absently, staring at the house.

"We should have done this before."

"Naturally, we make guests go in through the front door, but since you're practically family, anyway, I won't drop you all here," Suzanne said, pulling the car around to the side of the house. Ari was smiling his true grin – the flashier, toothier one was show – and Gennie sighed. She loved the Savannah house, with all its open space and privacy, but being on the grounds again only served to remind her of how clearly she didn't belong here, out on the island. This idyllic setting with all of its air and light and water was all too well suited for garden parties and social entertaining. Sitting in the gazebo with a book and a bag of sea-salt potato chips could quickly and sometimes unexpectedly turn into sweet tea and party dresses and doing her best to be charming. Just thinking about it made her feel stretched thin.

"All right, you all, let's go," Suzanne said, stopping the car. Ari got the bags out of the back of the SUV as a wave of hot, humid air hit Gennie in the face. It nearly stunned her after eight years away.

"Ari, Lynn will show you where you're staying. Gennie, you're in your old room," Suzanne said, turning to go into the house. "I'm going to go see how bad we're off tonight."

And there it was. Ari was off with Lynn in top chattery hostess form and Gennie was on her own in the garage. She slid upstairs, eager for the familiar territory of her own room, and stopped short in the doorway.

Looking back, she should have known better than to pack. Everything she had ever kept at the Savannah house was still there, untouched, with a bouquet of irises in a vase on her vanity table. Impulsively, she ran and jumped onto the big four-poster bed, letting the bedding fly up around her as the extra-soft mattress collapsed. When they were little, Carolyn had snuck into her room after bedtime and they would practice landing on the bed to create the greatest disorder possible. Gennie quickly re-straightened the sheets and the comforter so that her mother wouldn't notice, then went to her closet to see if there was anything in it that still fit. She startled at a knock on the door.

Ari poked his head into the room.

"Feel like getting out of your New York clothes?" he asked, bringing the checked bag into the room. "I already took all of my stuff out. I'm going to head downstairs. Your sister promised me a tour of the house."

"We used to say that you had to keep a string on your ears in case Carolyn talked 'em off," Gennie said, smiling a little. Ari grinned and put his arm around her waist, kissing her forehead.

"I like them, Gennie," he said. She nodded.

"I'm glad."

"The trick to cooking popular cuisine," Ari was saying as Gennie came downstairs later, "is to capture the local palate and creatively engage it."

Lynn and Suzanne were sitting on bar stools in front of the counter and range where Ari was working. As Gennie came into view, he picked a hot skillet off of a burner and dropped a quarter stick of butter onto it, sliding it around on the surface as it melted. Gennie's favorite teacher at the culinary school had had a motto: when you lose your train of thought, melt butter. Gennie smiled at the thought.

"Did you find everything to your liking, chef?" she asked. He had changed even since she had just seen him into his kitchen costume – tailored, white, heavy linen that could fend off hot grease, but mostly served to emphasize that none had hit him. The towel over his shoulder was for the untidy stuff.

"Half our kitchens at school weren't this well-equipped," he answered, smiling at her. He sloshed the butter around in the bottom of the pan, now, sprinkling flour through his fingers into it.

"What's he making?" Lynn asked.

"I never know until it's done," Gennie answered.

"That's not true," Ari said. "Not when we're on TV."

Gennie shrugged. That was accurate enough.

"Most international cuisine, when you get down to what people actually like to eat every day, falls into families," Ari said, recapturing his audience, "like the fugue in music."

"Dueling banjos," Lynn answered. Ari snorted a soft laugh.

"Illustrating both points elegantly," he said. "You put a primary grain into a hot, flat cooking implement, and in the northern US, you get pancakes. In the south you get cornbread. In France you get crepes, and in China you get bing." The pan rotated as the flour-butter mixture thickened, and he finally returned it to the range, reaching for a jug of milk. Gennie instinctively took the butter and the bag of flour out of his way, grabbing a second towel to clear the glass cooktop next to the skillet where a dusting of flour showed. She knew he would take half a step back to give her just enough space, without letting it look like she had pushed him out of the way and without interrupting his thesis.

"In the south, though, you like your breads to have substance. True southern cornbread has corn in it, and sugar in no smaller portion. These are lively, vibrant breads before you even think about adding anything to them. But then you do. Fruits, vegetables, meats, a veritable stew can be packed inside that primary grain bread under the sweeping title of half-moon pie, or turnover, or venturing further abroad, Italian calzones, Scotish bridies, German Strudels. These are the foods that we like to eat. They can't go wrong."

Gennie didn't strictly keep track of what went into Ari's foods – hers were hands that made connections happen and that kept what Ari was doing at the front and center of the audience's attention. He made a subtle motion as part of a hand gesture at a bowl of pecans that he had gotten out, and she found a cutting board and efficiently chopped them as he whisked a light batter and continued his thought.

"So, then, if we've already done everything that's worth doing, why do we send our hard-working sons and daughters to cooking school? Surely it's simply to learn high-brow, less palatable foods to prepare for people who like to think that they like foods in a better way than anyone else, is it not?"

Gennie stole a glance at her mother and sister as she slid the bowl of pecans under Ari's elbow and cleared several more ingredient containers. They were eating it up. Gennie took another quick cue and started slicing strawberries. Where was he going with this? How small would he want the fruit? Dinner portions in batter with pecans would be large enough to retain a coherent texture, but not as a feature.

"We like to think not. The purpose of learning how to cook is learning how to appreciate the qualities of a food that you want to bring out of it. A southern palate may be pleased by solid breads with plenty of lipids, but looking at other ideas about food can lead to great southern dishes that few have tried before."

The batter was bubbling up huge; whatever it was going to be, it had a lot of baking soda in it, Gennie thought, whisking the eggs away and replacing them with the bowl of strawberries.

"I'm going to need a bowl of ice," Ari said. She nodded. Cold would probably be to precondition the fruit; crushed ice for that. She had to remember where the plates were after she delivered the ice and watched him push the bowl of strawberries into the ice, then turn it over, leaving the strawberries in a bowl of ice. She missed the next part of his presentation, readying the plates. Dinner plates meant a decision: to garnish, or not to garnish? Ari didn't like mindless, inedible garnish, but she liked the way it looked on the plate, and in this case, she couldn't think of anything that was going to belong next to the pastry-bread-pancake he seemed to be concocting.

She had missed a second bowl of strawberries sitting on the

counter. As she set the plates down to prepare them, Ari set the second bowl next to a mortar and pestle – why did her momma have a mortar and pestle? – as though putting it out of the way. That was it, then. Strawberry sauce. She cleaned and crushed the strawberries, pouring the resulting pulp into a fresh glass bowl and placed it for him. Her stomach grumbled as she realized that this was going to be quite good.

The first pour of batter was already in the skillet and bubbling as he poured several spoonfuls of sugar into the strawberries, followed with a dollop of corn syrup. He crushed it all together again with a fork, continuing to talk to Lynn and Suzanne as Gennie began to rinse out used bowls and put them upside down in the sink. She grabbed a handful of silverware and put it into a glass to serve at a table, once Ari picked where they were going to eat. Chilled strawberries and pecans went into the only-slightly-mushy core of the cooked batter, and Ari folded it over on top of itself with a spatula, revealing a deep golden, nearly crispy exterior.

"Some other day, I'll tell you about cooking by smell, but the punch line is this – this has definitely gone right," Ari said. Lynn giggled and Suzanne nodded emphatically. Gennie's stomach grumbled again. The door to the garage opened, and – transported without thinking back to a previous time – Gennie flew out of the kitchen.

"Daddy!" she called.

"Hi, Sugar," he answered, setting down a briefcase to hug her. He smelled of cigar smoke and bourbon, like he always did in Savannah. They walked back to the kitchen arm-in-arm. "What's for dinner?"

"Whipped strawberry pancake turnovers with pecans and strawberry sauce," Ari answered.

"That's breakfast food," Gennie's daddy said gruffly.

"Not in Savannah, Georgia, when eaten sitting on a cool patio by the ocean at dusk," Ari said. "Then it's just a light, sweet, summer dinner."

"Supper," Gennie corrected happily. "Daddy, this is Ari. Ari, this is my daddy, Frank."

"Sir," Ari said, nodding sharply.

"Nice to meet you," Frank answered unconvincingly. This part Gennie had warned Ari about – it was her daddy's job to be skeptical of her boyfriend the first time they met. Anything else wouldn't be right.

Ari pulled the second pancake off of the skillet and poured the third.

"These are going to be finished in three minutes. Everyone should find the beverage of their choice and a chair they like outside. Gennie and I will serve everything," he said, winking at Gennie. He had rounded to get to three minutes; on set he would have told her the accurate number of seconds. Bread was tricky; it didn't hold heat like meat, especially with cold fruit in it. Whether or not the spectators knew it, this was going to be a feat of timing.

As she gave the sauce one more quick stir, she realized that the food was probably going to beat her family outside as they casually made for the refrigerator. She laughed.

"Just go. I'll get the drinks, too," she said. Lynn made a face at her, but surrendered the pitcher of sweet tea.

"Pancakes for dinner the first night?" Gennie teased Ari.

"It's the right call. It's hot out, but cooling off, and the sweet is just so Georgia," he said, pulling the third pancake and pouring the fourth.

"What do you know about Georgia?" she asked, bumping his hip. "Show off."

He smiled his real grin at her and portioned the sauce over the first three plates. She had glasses ready and poured tea for her mother and sister and a bourbon for her father, grabbing a pair of trays to carry the food outside.

"You want help?" Ari asked.

"I waited tables just like you," she said. "Besides, I'm hungry."

The sun had at least another hour to give as Gennie cleared her top tray of drinks and started handing out dinner plates, but Ari had been right about the cooling weather and the breeze. He stopped in the doorway behind her with the last tray of food.

"You didn't tell me I could have been cooking out here," he said, walking through the door after a pause.

"You'll get your chance, Hon," Suzanne said, waving a fork at him. "This is really good."

"Yum," Lynn agreed.

"It's a great breakfast," Frank said, smiling conspiratorially at Gennie when Ari wasn't looking.

"I'll make it up to you with a hearty breakfast in the morning, then, shall I, sir?" Ari said. Frank shrugged.

"No law says you have to cook the whole time you're here, son."

Ari nodded.

"I don't know what I'd do if I weren't cooking, though."

"It shows," Lynn said, laughing. "You ever write any of your recipes down?"

"Only for me," Gennie said. "Everything he makes is brand new every time."

Ari settled in on the end of the lawn chair that Gennie had chosen to recline on and for a few minutes there was just the sound of the water and distant sea birds as they ate.

"Dang," Lynn murmured. Suzanne grunted agreement. Ari smiled at his plate.

Gennie finally allowed herself to enjoy the meal. The pancake was light, sweet, and just begged to be eaten faster. The strawberries had survived cooking just the way she had hoped they would, which – mixed with the pecans – resulted in a perfect balance of hot and cold, soft and firm and crunchy, and fully sweet. She had missed just how much milk he had put into them; the bread wasn't just soft, but it was creamy and substantial at the same time. These types of textures and flavors were often mutually exclusive in the food that she had grown up with, but Ari knew no limitations. She watched him chew, taken once again with the muscular jawline and the quick eyes. He closed his eyes, tasting, and a muscle under his eye twitched. That was a mental note of something that he would have changed. If she tried, she could have guessed it, but tonight she didn't care to. Right this second, her world was a quiet, salty-smelling back porch at the Savannah house with a sweet, perfect supper, sitting just feet from the only man she knew who had the ability to make it.

The next morning, Gennie woke warm and happy, cocooned in a mountain of bedding with a cool breeze blowing down on her face from the ceiling fan. An instant later, her entire body jolted with a shot of adrenaline. She had overslept.

It took her several moments of bewildered wit-gathering to remember where she was, what she was doing there, and why the sun was already up.

"Momma!"

"Sugar, you had a long day, yesterday," Suzanne said as Gennie came storming downstairs.

"Momma, if I get off my routine at all, it's only going to be that much harder to get back onto it when we go home," Gennie said.

"Relax, Gennie. You've got a whole week off. Why not enjoy it?" Lynn called from the kitchen. Gennie's eyes got wide. It was the smell of breakfast that had woken her. She rounded the dining room into the den, from which she could see Lynn hovering behind Ari as he took a breakfast casserole out of the oven. Lynn was covered in flour or powdered sugar, one, and the kitchen was a wreck. Gennie just stared.

"Go on upstairs and get yourself presentable, Hon," Suzanne said from behind her. "Everything will be ready when you get done."

Gennie swallowed hard and stared for another moment, then forced herself to turn and walk back upstairs. In her room, she stood in front of the full-length mirror in her closet and took deep breaths. She was overreacting, she counseled herself. Not. That. Big. A. Deal. Her eyes stung, and she blinked hard.

"Today is going to suck," she said. They ruined it from the outset.

Gennie barely touched her breakfast, pulling it apart on her plate until her family finished eating, then bolting into the kitchen to put it down the disposal.

"You're coming, aren't you?" Ari asked, following Gennie back into the house with Lynn.

"Course I am," Lynn said over her shoulder to him.

"He was talking to me," Gennie said, vaguely remembering that they had talked about going to the market at breakfast.

"Why wouldn't you go?" Lynn asked. She looked at Ari, who opened his mouth and, as Gennie straightened to look at him, closed it again. He shrugged. Gennie cocked an eyebrow and held his eye for a minute.

"Oooh, she's got you buffaloed," Lynn said, laughing as she went to get her purse from the den. Ari came over to her and touched her arm.

"You're coming, though, aren't you?" he asked. She nodded. He wasn't about to just leave her at the house while he went off to the farmers' market without her. It pricked her a bit that he could even think it.

She still felt muddled and disorganized as she went back upstairs to try to find a pair of open-toed shoes for the market, and she grimaced a little at how her room smelled like dark and sweat now. That's what oversleeping smells like, and the inside of her head felt like her room smelled. She went and opened the windows, leaving the fan on to circulate air and dug through her bag for a moment before giving up and picking a different pair of sandals out of her closet. She closed her door behind her so that the air conditioning wouldn't try to cool her room all day and headed downstairs, dropping her sandals on the stairs in front of her one after the other to put them on. Ari was waiting for her; Suzanne and Lynn were already out in the garage.

"Sugar," Suzanne said over her shoulder as Gennie and Ari got into the car, "I'm having some ladies over tonight for an early dinner. I was going to have it catered, but if you don't mind, I'd rather have you show off. They're some dear friends of mine, and I know they'd be just green if they knew what a wonderful cook Gennie was dating."

"Chef," Gennie muttered under her breath.

"Wouldn't mind at all. I'll have to insist that we make it to the farmer's market today, though, so that I can see what I have to work with and plan a menu," Ari answered. "And I've been browsing your wine cellar – I've been very impressed, but there are a couple of bottles that I'd like to add as good all-arounds, if we got a chance."

Lynn laughed again.

"Better get more than a couple; when momma gets together with her lady-friends, they go through them."

"Hush," Suzanne replied, grinning. "You drink your fair share, at that." Lynn shrugged.

"So what are we having, then?" Lynn asked.

"Don't know. Depends on what smells good," Ari answered. It drove their segment producer mad, some days; he would have had a recipe planned for days, and would suddenly turn up with something else entirely that he had bought at the market on his way in to work with Gennie. Some random ingredient would spark something for him, and he would go off in some complete new direction, usually requiring different equipment and a new camera arrangement – from time to time, entirely on the fly. Gennie made the food work, and Sebrine made the footage work, and that was that, but it didn't stop Sebrine from pulling her hair out every time it happened.

"What happened to duck breast with mango? Duck breast with mango was good. It was all on the stove," Sebrine would say.

"The shallots were calling to me," Ari would say. "I need a cast-iron skillet and you're going to want to watch them coming out of the oven. And a butane torch."

And the kitchen area of the set would erupt as they tried to re-make the whole segment. Ari would stand peacefully in the middle of it all, putting his hands on ingredients and smelling them, or rubbing this or that powder between his fingers, just dreaming. The producers only tolerated it because these were his best segments, the ones that got internet activity up and that sponsors wanted to be associated with. '*Ari's had a lightning bolt*,' some PA would whisper in the hallway as Gennie hustled by with Cuban yellow grape tomatoes. She smiled despite herself, sitting in the back seat of the SUV, at the chaos he could unwittingly unleash chasing a lightning bolt.

"Couldn't you keep him away from the market until after the show?" Sebrine had asked Gennie once. "Who in their right mind is shopping for food at that hour, anyway?"

Gennie hadn't told her that Ari wasn't shopping for food at the market at that hour; he had made arrangements with vendors at the market *the day before* to purchase the freshest food available at four o'clock that morning.

The Savannah market didn't bear a strong resemblance to the various markets around Manhattan that Gennie and Ari frequented, but it was vibrant and full of food and people, just the way it was supposed to be.

"You want to get lost on purpose?" Ari whispered in Gennie's ear. Gennie sighed and nodded.

"Yeah."

Suzanne and Lynn stopped at one of the first stalls to chat with a shopper that Suzanne recognized, and Ari and Gennie slipped past into a crowd of people, taking a quick turn out of sight. Ari ran his fingers down the inside of her wrist to find her hand, weaving his fingers through hers. Then: "Spinach!"

Three stalls later, Ari already had an armload of bags of produce: three kinds of lettuce, spinach, asparagus, spring onions, and a locally-bred hybrid tomato that the seller assured them was the optimal blend of tangy and sweet, and that Ari diagnosed by smell as perfect for the garden salad he had in mind.

"How long has it been since we've thought about courses? And feeding a group of people?" Ari asked. Gennie had to smile as he dashed to the next stall.

"Since school, I guess. Your parents don't eat very much," Gennie said.

"And our friends don't eat at four," Ari finished their inside joke.

"I'm sorry I was short with you this morning," Gennie said, wrapping her arm around his and holding on to his shoulder as she leaned her cheek against it.

"This trip was supposed to be harder for me than it was for you," Ari joked gently, putting his head on top of hers. "I'm sorry this morning didn't go right. It wasn't what I meant to happen."

Gennie nodded.

"I know."

That was it. The sky brightened, the air lightened, and a breeze swept through the market, flapping banners and awnings, and they went on.

"I need a protein," Ari told her. "Or better, two."

The kitchen was in rare form as the ladies started to arrive. Five courses, appetizer through dessert, were in various stages of preparation, and Gennie was elated. This was what Ari excelled at, even more than showmanship. The salads were ready except for the tomato – kept separate until the last moment to keep the acid from impacting the rest of the flavors prematurely. The fish course was plated, except for the fish itself, which was raw and ready to go into a pan to cook the moment the salads hit the table. The beef was slow-cooking in the oven at 175 degrees, the last time Gennie had looked at it, to be at just the right degree of heated and cooked-through at just the right moment, for the fourth course. Potatoes were boiling, onions were chopped, garlic was pressed, and yet the kitchen was the identity of cleanliness and Ari was radiant in his white chef's smock. Gennie was on her fourth kitchen towel, but no one would count those at the end of the night.

"Ladies," Ari started from the head of the table as Gennie stirred a white sauce that had to thicken and then cool before it was served. "The first course is ready, if you'll take your seats."

The ladies ooh-ed and aah-ed over the table settings – Gennie had had to go back into town at the last minute before they started cooking to get sterling-silver candlesticks, because all her mother had was crystal, and it wasn't the setting that Ari had in mind, when he looked at it – and made their even-paced way to the table, the soprano voices rising and falling in conversation that Gennie hardly bothered to track. Someone was married, someone was dead, someone was dating, and someone else *should* be dating by now. Gennie dished out the tomatoes and poured the honey garlic vinaigrette over top of the plates. She pulled her gloves out of the drawer where she had stashed them when she got home, and went to stand behind Ari with the first two plates.

He introduced the starter course with all due formality and embellishment, including the fact that all of the ingredients on the table had been attached to their respective plants just yesterday. Gennie smiled to herself as she served the first two plates – serve from the left, clear from the right – the food had *probably* been picked yesterday, with the exception of the white wine vinegar, the wine itself, and the pecans that she knew for a fact had to be dried before they were edible, and then the items that didn't come from plants in the first place, but who was really counting those? It was the spectacle that Ari captured, and it was the spectacle that people watched him for.

Ari was already back in the kitchen as she finished up serving.

"Not much food, is it, dear?" her mother's best friend asked Gennie.

"It's because there's so much coming. If no one ate the dessert because they had eaten too much of everything else, there wouldn't be any point in making it, would there?" Gennie answered, smiling. "Bon appetite, ladies."

In the kitchen, still in view of the dining table, the frenzy resumed. Ari was peeling boiling-hot potatoes in his bare hand, the clever fingers making their way around the potato with nuanced speed as the peeler worked its magic, and Gennie was chopping them as quickly as they left his hands into soft cubes that would go into a baked potato dish sometime in the middle of the second course. The last potato she put into cheesecloth as Ari moved on to cooking the fish in a pre-heated skillet. She put water-absorbent paper on top and underneath the cheesecloth and pounded the potato with a flat mallet a couple of times, crushing the potato completely, and then swapped out the paper, pushing more and more water out of the potato as the soft smell of mild fish filled the kitchen. Gennie switched on the range hood fan to keep the smell from getting overpowering as the fish rapidly cooked. She didn't need to pay attention to the diners to know that the food was being appreciated, so she didn't. She and Ari had both sampled all of the food multiple times through its preparatory process, and she knew it was amazing. At the end of the night, despite having worked the whole time, she and Ari would have eaten more than anyone at the table.

The convection oven was already at 450 degrees, and when she was satisfied that she couldn't pull any more water out of her potato, she peeled it out of the cheesecloth and put it into the oven. She looked at Ari. He touched a plate, feeling rather than seeing her eyes, and she looked out at the table. The salad plates were empty enough to start collecting them, and it would push the chattier diners into finishing up. The fish was ready; the round two window was open.

Gennie got various 'thank you, hon's and 'that was lovely's from the table as she cleared the plates, and then Ari was back at the table introducing round two. The table silenced as he explained the parts of the dish and a quick reasoning behind the design decisions he had made for the course. There was too much going on for him to indulge his audience the way he normally would have, so he left Gennie to get the plates out and returned to the kitchen to get the white sauce settled and the potatoes in the much-hotter second oven. Stacked ovens and a convection oven, and he had still run out. Gennie was pouring wine as she heard the stand mixer start. That dried potato couldn't be ready yet, she thought. She needed to get water on to boil.

The blackberry sauce was in the refrigerator from about two hours ago, so Gennie pulled that out then filled a pot with pre-heated water and put it on to the range to boil. The baby carrots and asparagus that she had prepped earlier went into a basket above that to steam as the water heated. Ari touched his shoulder to hers as he peeked at the blackberry sauce.

"Twelve and a half minutes on the potatoes, forty-five seconds on the dried potato, two minutes on the pasta, and..." he paused to stir and spoon out enough of the white sauce to watch it drip, "ninety seconds on the white sauce."

She nodded, going to stand in front of the convection oven, counting down from thirty. The potato crumbled apart in her hands as she pulled it out and walked across the kitchen to add it to the pasta mix, checking to make sure that Ari was adding the parmesan to the white sauce. He had that, so she waited the minute for the pasta ball to firm, then pulled it off the dough hook and set it on the flour-covered baking mat next to the stand mixer.

"Who has these, anymore?" Ari asked, bringing over the hand-crank pasta roller. "I thought the culinary world had gone to extrusion-only pasta."

Gennie acknowledged the joke distractedly, going back to check on the carrots and asparagus.

Ari pulled the cooler oven open, sticking a fork into it and pulling out one of the thin slices of beef. He returned and dipped the beef into the blackberry sauce, offering Gennie the first bite, then finishing it himself. Her eyes widened. He focused for a minute, then went to get a lime out of the refrigerator. *Are you kidding?* she almost asked, then thought about it and laughed. Yup.

"You've got it," she said. He touched a bowl where he had left a stick of butter and an assortment of spices – Gennie smelled rosemary and nutmeg – and started plating the meat. She microwaved the butter sauce and was ready with it by the time he was ready to pull the vegetables from over the boiling water.

Leaving him to finish the plating work, Gennie made her way out to the table to fill the next set of wine glasses and take the couple of plates that were ready.

"Ari, will you come cook for me every night?" the woman from two doors down called as Gennie took her plate and returned to the kitchen with it, making a quick effort to rinse and sort the used dishes and utensils before she went back for the next plates.

"I'd rather teach you how to make meals like this on your own," Ari answered, wiping the edge of a plate to clear the blackberry sauce he had dripped.

"And why would I want to be making food when I could be eating it?" the woman replied merrily, tipping back her wine glass.

Ari was using a stiff brush to coat the vegetables with the butter sauce as Gennie returned to the kitchen with the last plates, and she followed him back to the table to wait out his presentation of the next course. So far, she was nearly certain that they had hit all of their windows, but the starch course was concerning her. She would have put this one second or third, not forth, and all of the potatoes were coming finished faster than the ladies were eating. Meat held heat better than starch did, and she thought there was a good chance that the potatoes might end up getting served cold.

As usual, though, Ari was right and she was wrong. The ladies continued to chat, the wine continued to disappear, and the food consumption slowed slightly, but the potatoes coming out of the oven were five-hundred degrees, and it took every bit of the time required both to get the pasta rolled, rested, and cooked and for the ladies to finish the beef course before the baked potatoes reached a palatable temperature. Again, Gennie and Ari were passing each other in the kitchen as he assembled the dish with a sprinkle of paprika on top – for color, Gennie thought, at least as much as for flavor – and went to introduce it.

And that was it. The last course was cake – not literally – and Gennie was finally able to take a moment to breathe and consider what they had pulled off. On TV, they just generated clips, maybe ten minutes at a time, on how to prepare one item that was generally pretty simple and unadventurous. Here, though, Ari was trying anything he felt like, just doing what the ingredients seemed to want him to do. She smiled, picking through the various leftovers. It was all amazing. He never put a foot wrong, so to speak, in the kitchen, and somehow it still amazed her.

"Well?" he asked softly, returning from the table. She fed him a caramelized potato and nodded.

"Ten."

He shook his head.

"White sauce should have cooled longer, fish was fileted too thick, blackberry sauce sat too long," he said. She frowned playfully.

"Ten."

He shook his head again, grinning his real grin, now.

"You're too easy."

"You want to start on the dessert?" she asked. He shook his head.

"We've blitzed them hard. Let's let them catch up."

She grinned at him and grabbed a spoon to scrape potatoes out of the ceramic container he had cooked them in.

"Darlin', these noodles are different. Where did you buy them?" Suzanne called from the table.

"They're potato noodles," Ari called back, looking at Gennie. "You want to go sit with them?"

She shook her head.

"I'm going to get more of the cleaning done. You go ahead."

He deserved the accolades he got, there was no doubt. There certainly wasn't any part of her that wished that people would recognize her on the street in New York the way they did him. There was just something about the way that he would go from being Ari and Gennie to just Ari when people were telling him how much they liked his food and his cooking or just him personally that was soft and sad for Gennie. At the beginning, he had tried to drag her into the lime light with him. He had made her go on camera with him for the last shot of a segment, and he would introduce her at the market to fans, but she desperately hated the patronizing way that people would smile at her, recognizing her as the hanger-on that she was. She didn't mind being a hanger-on; she just hated people pretending she didn't know, or that she didn't know that they knew.

So she washed dishes. Or looked at kale. Whatever was most convenient and most satisfying method of getting out of that melting spotlight that Ari just sizzled in.

Fifteen minutes later or so, Gennie served coffee and Ari invited the ladies to sit out on the back porch and enjoy the breeze. Gennie pulled the rest of the bounty of berries that Ari had bought out of the freezer.

"Berries," he had said, standing in front of the first fruit stall. Gennie had raised her eyebrows at him.

"Fresh berries from Georgia. We have to use those," he said. She shrugged.

"You know what you do with Georgia berries?" she asked.

"Syrup, glaze, dressing, sorbet, garnish..." he started.

"Eat them," she had cut in with mock scorn.

So he had frozen them. Taken two liters of fresh berries and put them straight into the freezer. If she hadn't known for sure how well they were going to turn out, she would have been upset about it.

Ari returned from outside to pull out the berries that he thought were the best garnishes, and Gennie dumped the rest – with a sigh – into the blender. To the crystalized fruit mixture, Ari added lemon juice, lime juice, sugar, and fresh mint that he crushed between his hands and tore to miniscule pieces before introducing it.

"No water, no cream, just fruit and sugar," he said as he dipped a spoon into the blend. Gennie had been a bit apprehensive about adding mint to fruit – they kept them strictly separate in chewing gum, after all – but as Ari held his hand under her chin and to let her try the mix, the brilliance of it dawned on her. The mint, in that mix, didn't taste like mint. Instead, it added a breathlessness to the sweetness of the berries and the tang of the lemon and lime.

"That's summer," she said before the words had even turned into meaning in her mind. He laughed spontaneously, grabbing a serving spoon and quickly distributing the mix into the daiquiri glasses Gennie had waiting.

"You aren't going to try it?" she asked. He kissed her on the forehead quickly as he worked.

"That reaction is everything I could ever ask for. Even if I hated it, I wouldn't change a thing."

Gennie covered her mouth to hide the blush, and he kissed her jaw.

"Come sit with us."

He was gone. Frozen desserts were ready whenever, but when they were ready, they were *ready*. She followed musing happily over the mixture of flavors still on her palate, taking a chair at the patio table and letting Ari hand her a glass. The tiny dessert spoons portioned out the bites to exactly the right size such that she got all of the flavor without freezing her mouth, but she was impatient to get through all of it before it started to thaw out and turn into juice.

As she finally conceded and drank the last tablespoon of pulp and juice out of the bottom of her glass, she became aware of the fact that conversation was swirling around her. Ari was certainly at the center of it, his ringmaster smile beaming at the women as they peppered him with questions and their desserts melted.

Gennie just watched him. She was genuinely proud. No one else could work a crowd the way Ari could, when there was food involved. And as much character as he might put on, in public, none of it was a lie. It was just turning up the wattage on his natural self. She would find herself sitting at the dinner table comparing her Ari with the television Ari, almost smug that he didn't think he had to *sell* her those traits. He just let her find them as they were.

As she sat on the back porch of the Savannah house, it hit her again. That smile, that wink, the way his tongue emerged past his teeth when he answered a comment in laughter – these were all things about her Ari, but things that only she could actually recognize.

"Gennie," Lynn said sharply, snagging her attention. Gennie looked at her, unbraced.

"So what's it like to be the also-ran in the show?" Lynn asked. Gennie was still unprepared.

"What?"

"The replaceable one. What are you going to do when he doesn't need you anymore?"

It was supposed to be teasing, and Gennie knew it, but she couldn't bring herself to answer it in fun.

"I make his cooking work," Gennie said. "He wouldn't be able to do what he does without me."

"Without *someone*," Lynn corrected, grinning widely. "I helped him just fine this morning."

"I'm sure you aren't as good at it as she is," Suzanne said.

"I'm sure I'd rather be eating than cooking," the woman from down the street said. The other ladies laughed.

"You couldn't do what I do," Gennie said, still looking at Lynn.

"I'm sure she could learn it, sweetie," Suzanne said passively, turning to ask her best friend about some benefit the other woman was planning the next month. Gennie's eyes didn't leave Lynn. Lynn shrugged.

"What?" she mouthed at Gennie.

"You couldn't do what I do," Gennie said again, just for Lynn to hear.

"You mix things, darlin," Lynn said and shrugged. "Don't blow it all out of proportion."

"Excuse me," Gennie said, her temper bubbling out of control again. She left her glass on the patio table and went inside, heading straight upstairs to her room, seeking refuge.

Unfortunately, she had forgotten to come upstairs and close her windows after they came back from the market, and her room was swelteringly hot. She snorted at the windows and slammed them shut one after the other, ignoring that the lace curtain got stuck in the second one. She stripped out of her cooking clothes and found something lighter to wear, but the heat didn't allow for much relief. She sat down on her bed and looked at her reflection in her vanity mirror.

"Grow up," she whispered at herself. After a few minutes, she had steeled herself. "Just grow up."

She walked back downstairs and out onto the patio, but mainly just sat and played with her spoon until the ladies decided it was time to head home.

"You want to go for a walk on the beach?" Ari asked.

"We haven't got a beach," Gennie answered. "Just swamp."

"That's the ocean over there, isn't it?" Ari protested.

"Just swamp," Gennie reaffirmed.

"Smells bad, too," Lynn told him. Suzanne nodded.

"I'm going to go turn on the news," Suzanne said, standing. Eventually everyone migrated into the den where they could sit in the air conditioning for the rest of the evening and listen to someone else talk.

The next morning, Gennie woke to the familiar, jarring sensation of hatred for her alarm clock. As she sleepily considered it, she wasn't sure which was worse – waking up having overslept or waking up on time. She dozed in the consideration and jolted at a knock on the door.

"Mmmwha?" she answered. Ari stuck his head in the doorway.

"Babe, we need to get going. I've got a lot I want to do today," he said. She raised her eyebrows at him, or at least she thought she did.

"Dinner tonight?" he asked. She shook her head, frustrated.

"You're not makin' any sense," she said, her belle coming through strong without a coherent filter on it. Ari sighed.

"You really weren't listening?"

Gennie swallowed hard past the dry spot at the back of her throat and closed one eye at him in annoyance.

"Linda's husband is coming tonight," he said, as though

that explained it all. She rolled over in bed, pulling the comforter up over her shoulder.

"Linda's husband is an executive for a cooking network based in Atlanta," Ari said crossly. "He's coming tonight to watch me cook because she thinks I should have my own show."

Gennie sat up in bed.

"She what?"

"I tried to get you to talk to me about this last night," Ari said, exasperated, as they browsed food stalls at the market. They had finally ducked Suzanne and Lynn, but they weren't getting a lot of shopping done.

"Why would you even consider it? Going from network television in New York City to some local thing in Atlanta?" Gennie asked, digging through a pile of squash with perhaps more vigor than necessary.

"Because I would go from a twice-a-week appearance on a morning show to *my own show*."

"Atlanta?"

He shook his head at her, handing cash over to the stall vendor.

"You can't fool me. I can see in your face how much you love this place," he said. She looked at him, wide-eyed.

"You don't even know, do you? Every time you're not actively thinking about how unhappy you are, you have this dumb smile on your face that I've never seen before," he said. "I would consider working in Atlanta out of my own self-interests, but you are happy here."

Gennie turned her back, going on to the next stall. He caught her shoulder.

"Please," he said earnestly. "Please. Just give yourself a chance to like the idea. We're not committed to anything; it's just dinner."

She sighed and collapsed against his chest, and he held her with some apparent relief.

"I'm sorry," she said. "It's a great opportunity, and you should consider it."

"We should consider it," he echoed. "No matter what, we're going to make it work, okay?"

She nodded.

"I know. I'm just..." she sighed. "I'm tired."

He squeezed her and pushed her back over her own feet, running his free hand through her hair.

"I know."

"So tonight," Ari said to the five people sitting at the patio table as he stood in the outdoor kitchen, "I thought that instead of trying to impress you with what I cook, I'd like to impress upon you *how* I cook. That's what television is about on all levels, after all, and then at the end of the day, *what* gets cooked should be good, should be appetizing in both appearance and concept, and should be something that people who watch can actually *do*."

"So," he said, and snapped, "let's get started."

Gennie pulled the top post-it off of a stack of staggered post-its stuck just out of sight behind the cabinet. *Mash tomatoes, drain, and put them on to boil, brown ground bison.*

The Ari snap was a thing. People snapped at him on the street. It was generally believed to be a charismatic emphasis, and Ari was happy with people thinking that that's what it was, but it was actually a way for him to dynamically time complex preparation steps without having to otherwise cue Gennie. He wrote out the list of items that needed to be done on individual post-it notes, then, instead of cuing by touch or with verbal countdowns, he'd say something emphatic and snap.

"People ask me where I get my ideas for foods. I'm always trying new things, they tell me, and they don't understand what muse I'm relying on for inspiration. It's actually a lot simpler than most people think. People get overwhelmed by food because they don't know how it's going to turn out when they finish."

He took a step to the side to start stirring the tomatoes, reaching for a turnstyle of dry seasonings.

"For example, making your own tomato sauce. You go to the store and there are at least a hundred varieties to pick from, and they're all a giant mystery, and you pick one that you hope you remember you liked last time. People look at a pot of boiling tomatoes and see the same conundrum.

"But the idea that you can't know how your food is going to turn out is *not* true," he said, snapping again. *Pasta. Make dough. Boil water.*

The stand mixer had been moved outside for the event. Gennie moved on, leaving the browned meat in the skillet next to the range to drain.

"There are only a very few food qualities that you can taste that you can't smell. While I normally cook with fresh herbs, I want to put together a meal from scratch – one that you probably eat from time to time, anyway – and to look at how do you make that meal taste the way you want it to taste *today* – while only using ingredients you should be able to find on your normal grocery run."

Chop tomatoes. Grate mozzarella.

Gennie had mostly lost track of the narration from the ground bison, instead immersing herself in the sounds and smells of cooking traditional, American food. No unnecessary flair, no huge leaps of experimentation. This was the stuff that she imagined herself cooking when she packed up her car and drove to New York in the first place. Her hands went through the familiar motions associated with the tasks Ari needed her to do, and in between, she moved things to be more relevant; ingredients he was going to need next closer to hand, things he was momentarily done with further away. Clean off the countertop, sweep used utensils. He was certainly telling the truth about the work necessary to do what he was doing, but she made it look effortless and professional.

Oven to 350, coat pan with olive oil, caramelize onions.

The smell of the tomato sauce simmering made her stomach growl. Ari was away with the pasta. She stirred the sauce a couple of quick times, then poured olive oil into a skillet to heat and started chopping onions. Enough volume for flavor and texture variety, but not so big as to be a distracting texture.

This was their show. The same dance that they always did, getting everything done, but instead of planning 9 minutes of content, Ari worked for 30 minutes of solid direction from the thesis to the food to the commercial break opportunities. It might have only been lasagna, but it was mesmerizing as far as Gennie was concerned.

Ari had rolled the noodles paper thin and cooked them, and the sauce came off the stove directly onto the lasagna like icing a cake. Fourteen layers, including one that was three quarters of an inch of bison and ricotta cheese.

"Bake for fifteen minutes to heat through and get everything melted together right, and you've got yourself an inexpensive high quality meal that turns out exactly how you'd hoped it would," Ari said. "Now, because I wouldn't like to disappoint anyone by being underwhelming, we also have an Umbrian flatbread appetizer that Gennie snuck into the oven ten minutes ago, an Italian loaf that I've let rise for the last two hours to go in with the lasagna, and a mint gelato for dessert."

Gennie pulled the flatbread out of the oven and set it on the counter for him, making one last sweep of the cooking and preparation surfaces to make sure that the shot was spotless.

Linda's husband, Lee, raised his hand and waved Ari over.

"Linda told me that you missed the whole meal last night. Come eat with us; we'll talk."

Gennie's pulse picked up. She didn't have place settings for seven set out, and she was quite certain that the table wasn't big enough for seven – just six. Ari seemed to share none of her concerns, though, so as he pulled the sixth chair out for himself, Gennie breezed into the kitchen to collect the additional two place settings. She would make it work. When she returned, Air stood to get another chair.

"Here," Lee said, moving over. "Let the lovely young Genevieve sit next to her mother; you come sit next to me, and we'll talk business." Ari nodded.

"Sure, but keep in mind that it's Gennie's business, too. We work as a pair."

Lee laughed.

"Son, I know for a fact that the station would air nothing but snow, if it weren't for my assistant. I wouldn't make that mistake, I assure you."

Gennie got Ari's place setting worked out and went to tend to her own, suddenly nervous.

They were good. She knew that. But here she sat at a table with a man who held an opportunity that Ari wanted, and there was nothing more she could do to influence his opinion. All that was left was the food, and he would make his judgment.

"You've got the charisma, can't nobody deny you that," Lee said as Air sat back down. "You'd be a lock for the 35-45 demographic that are interested in cooking shows. Tell me about what you're doing now."

Gennie listened passively as Lee and Ari discussed the ins and outs of the show up in New York, intentionally keeping her mind away from the conversation while keeping an eye on the stove to get the main course served as it finished up. The thin layers of the lasagna combined with the chopped tomatoes kept the entree from taking on a heavy, too-solid feel to it that would have been burdensome in the evening heat, and the bread, torn apart and dipped in individual saucers of garlic oil, felt Mediterranean and made Gennie wish that she were dressed for such a meal, rather than wearing her kitchen garb. She was sorely looking forward to the gelato.

As silverware started to scrape plates and Lynn finished the last of the bread, Ari stood.

"I've arranged for our dessert to be at the gazebo this evening, so that we can listen to the ocean as we eat. Gennie and I will go and prepare the gelato if you will kindly make your way over."

Gennie had spent Ari's bread-making time decorating the gazebo as per his instructions, with oil lamps and fresh flowers from the market – giant lilies and potted orchids – that had made the air smell cool and sweet even in the heat of the afternoon. She had crushed rose petals into hurricane bowls to augment the scent and had cut water lilies into other bowls to serve as centerpieces of the cafe-tables that Ari had asked be brought from the front garden back to the gazebo for the occasion. She had lit the lamps when the doorbell had sounded, so they had at least another two and a half hours to burn before they would need more oil.

Gennie followed Ari into the house then, impulsively, ran upstairs to her room to snatch a loose-fitting sundress out of her bag, ripping it over her head and running back downstairs. Ari looked up from his task as she re-entered the kitchen, and paused, his hand suspended over a partially portioned glass dish of gelato. His face softened from its normal work formality and focus as he looked her over, resting at her eyes.

"Wish you could do that more," he said softly. Gennie blushed.

"I bought it for this trip," she said not wanting to admit how much she had wanted him to see her like this and how desperately she had been fighting not to cave to the impulse. He smiled with just his mouth – no teeth, no dazzle, no sell – and sighed. He twisted his mouth to the side and motioned with his head to the glass pedestal bowls. She nodded. There was still work to finish.

When they got out to the gazebo, Gennie was too occupied to notice the aspect of her earlier work. The conversation had drifted back to local affairs and Lee didn't make an effort to bring it back to business. Ari engaged the group for a while, then joined Gennie at one of the built-in stone benches at the back of the gazebo. It had grown fully dark, and he squeezed her shoulders.

"Better than I could have imagined. You know the balance of the structure here way better than I do," he said. She shrugged under his arm a little harder and looked up at the burning lights for the first time. Suspended between the individual posts of the gazebo, they gave the ceiling a flickering orange nature that looked like the sunset on a calm sea. The air was crisp with the smell of the flowers, and she sighed, putting her head into the concavity where his shoulder met his chest.

"I wish that this was what life looked like," she murmured. He squeezed her, settling a little lower so that her head hit the deepest part of the hollow and his waist curved alongside her hip.

She must have drifted further than she thought, because the next space of awareness came in deep darkness, the oil lamps illuminating stubbornly black plants around the gazebo and insects singing a sleep-inducing chorus at the moon.

"Thank you sir," Ari said, making sure that Gennie was awake before he stood.

"I'm convinced by the persona and I'm convinced by the food, but I think that what might be more interesting, if you would be willing to consider it, would be a stress test of sorts. We have plenty of chefs who can cook a prepared, scripted meal. I've thought for a while that a chef who can cook under pressure, and still be entertaining and *successful* at preparing a meal would be a popular addition to our lineup."

The rest of the occupants of the gazebo were quiet as Ari considered.

"What did you have in mind?" he asked.

"I've got a production staff who would have to sign on to make a pilot, no matter what I say. If I can get them all here Friday night, I want you to throw everything you have at them – live. You let them figure out which parts they would want to put into a show, you just do a show, flour and eggs all the way to clearing the dishes. What is that, about five hours?"

Ari thought for a long minute; Gennie found that she wasn't really breathing.

"How many people are we talking about?"

Lee pursed his lips.

"Fifteen plus the five of us. I won't make you eat with us."

"If Suzanne wouldn't mind playing hostess to that many for that long," Ari said, "I'd want everyone here at two without any expectation of leaving before nine."

Lee nodded, looking at Suzanne. Gennie's momma shrugged expansively.

"No different than a regular Friday night, Lee."

"Don't let me over-sell you," Lee said, offering his hand to Ari. Ari took it firmly, grinning his show grin.

"I'm not at all worried," he said. Gennie stood.

"Tell your producer to bring a still camera for the portfolio for the pilot," Gennie said. "I'll get him the shots he needs to sell the show."

Lee cocked an eyebrow at Gennie, amused.

"Of course."

Lee and Linda made the socially appropriate farewells to Gennie's family and Lee and Ari shook hands once more, then the evening was over.

"Lynn, could I impose on you to bring the dishes back inside?" Ari asked. Lynn shrugged.

"Whatever," she said. He collected them on a platter and handed them to her as Suzanne and Frank watched.

"You've got guts, son," Frank said as Lynn headed back up to the house. Ari waited for more, but that was all.

"Um. Thank you," he answered. Frank nodded and Gennie smiled at him.

"Thank you, Daddy," she said, hugging him.

"I'm going to go call Betsy," Suzanne said, beaming. She kissed Ari's cheek, then bustled up to the house, followed by Frank at his own leisurely pace.

"Can we talk?" Ari asked Gennie. She took a breath of the thick, scented night air.

"We can go down to the pier," she said. "The tide will be in."

Ari took her arm, tucking it tight against his body so that her side warmed against his, then stopped.

"Just a second," he said. "I'll be right back."

He jogged up to the house, leaving her in the fading orange shadows beside the gazebo. She wrapped her arms around each other, staring up at the moon, slowly meandering to the gap in the woods where the wooden walkway to the pier started. Shortly, Ari rejoined her, wearing long, loose jeans and a white linen shirt that was open at the chest.

"When in Savannah," he said, taking her arm back up.

"What do you know about Georgia?" she replied, pressing against him.

The sea breeze that was making its way along the path was cool and Gennie put her hand up onto her captive arm for Ari to hold.

"The board is loose, there," she warned him.

"I would die, walking this way in the dark by myself, wouldn't I?" he asked.

"Yes," she told him, smiling into his sleeve.

He was so happy that he was practically purring, unable to keep any particular pose even as they walked, rubbing her arm then putting his head on top of hers. The pier was on the other side of the narrow band of woods, beyond a low-lying marsh that had filled with water at the tide. Gennie's daddy's boat made soft nighttime knocking noises against its dock, and Gennie went to sit at the far end of the pier, pulling off her sandals and dropping her feet into the water. Ari leaned against the railing, watching her.

"You really do look like you belong here," he said. She smiled down at the water, watching it drift up and down her calves. This corner of the pier hadn't been footed right, and it had dropped down some, making it her favorite place to sit because sitting anywhere else along the pier, only her toes would reach the water.

"It's hardly ever like this," she told him, breathing the briny water indulgently, "but this comes close to making it worth it."

"You look amazing," he said. She turned around and looked at him.

"You're not so bad yourself," she said, teasing to cover the awkwardness of how true it was. He smiled at her as she held his eye, then he turned.

"I'm sorry. I know I should be here, but I can't think about anything else but Friday night."

He stood and went to lean on the thick round post that the

boat was moored to. Gennie watched him for a moment.

"So talk to me," she said.

"He's talking about a reality show. I want to do amazing things that they've never even thought of before. Six courses, maybe seven. Shellfish, beef, *venison!*, poultry..." he cast about, looking out over the ocean, "whole barley and molasses over duck; cantaloupe- and mint-marinated filet cut beef – bison – both... Bourbon stir-fried shrimp and potato on long-grain wild rice..."

"Mango and orange," Gennie said. "You have to do mango and orange."

"Mango, orange, and honey over stuffed quail," he said, as though her voice had been a part of his own thoughts.

"I don't know where to get quail," Gennie said. "We'll have to ask around."

Ari looked at her with intensity.

"Anything. Everything. All at once. Wine, cheese, tea, coffee, pastries, hors d'oevres... Like a giant final that I can't fail."

Gennie grinned at his fervency. He looked at her and laughed.

"We can't fail. Do you know what I would be like without you?"

"Yes," she said grinning. "You'd point at an empty bowl and be completely lost."

He shook his head, agreeing.

"Do you think that there is anything we can't do? Honestly. I've never found the limit; if it's out there, you have to tell me."

"Nothing," she said. The water rolling up her legs hit the pier and splashed through. She flew off the deck, shrieking laughter as she brushed the water off her dress. He strode directly to her and folded her shoulders against his chest, holding her tight as she laughed. She put her arms around his chest, hard, laughing herself exhausted, then they just rocked for a few minutes.

The night air kept pushing her skirt back against her legs,

and she shivered. He kissed her head.

"Let's go," he said, kissing her temple. "I can't stand still anymore."

He wove his fingers through hers and they walked back up the path, Gennie pointing out the gap in the boards. He stopped her just short of the light of the back door, holding her shoulders square to him. She watched him patiently as he looked at her face. His thumb traced her jawline, resting at the corner of her mouth. Her fingers tingled. He tilted her face up to his and kissed her mouth, sweet and soft.

"I love you," he whispered.

"I love you, too," she answered, burying herself into his chest.

Later, sitting up in bed with a book, Gennie's mind fluttered too much to either read or sleep. Their first kiss had been sophomore year, and the exchange of 'I love you's had come early junior year, but he still had the ability to electrify her. Surely one day it would get old and routine, but it hadn't yet, and she snuggled against her pillows in the deliciousness of the sensation. She finally gave up on the book – she hadn't turned the page in twenty minutes – and turned off the lamp beside her bed, but it would be a number of hours before she could quiet her thoughts enough for sleep.

"I don't think that boy slept at all last night," Suzanne said the next morning over bagels. Gennie raised her eyebrows at her.

"He was pacing out in the garden when I got up, and your Daddy said that he fixed oatmeal for both of them before your Daddy headed to work this morning."

Gennie shrugged.

"He's taking it seriously," she said. "It's a big opportunity."

"Just make sure he doesn't get too caught up in it and forget why y'all came," Suzanne said, turning the page of her newspaper.

"Hmm?" Gennie asked, looking at her hard.

"He needs to talk to your Daddy first," Suzanne said meaningfully without looking up from her article.

Gennie mostly lost the next two days. There was food, there were practice dishes, there was shopping for food, and there was eating. The eating was so infused with the rest of the days that she lost track of what she had eaten when, and what it had actually *been* that she had eaten.

Thursday afternoon, they were cooking out on the back patio and Ari was in his 'when in Savannah' shirt. Lynn had been flirting with him transparently. Gennie wasn't sure if she was being unfair in characterizing what her momma had been doing as the same.

"You're going to make a great TV star," Lynn said.

"He already is a TV star," Gennie muttered, scrubbing a potato.

"I want to try the quail dish again," Ari said. "It didn't turn out the way I expected, last time."

They had found a quail farm outside of a tiny town called Sylvester that had sent them forty birds by truck. Gennie had been up late the night before prepping them. She nodded at Ari and went into the kitchen to get another pair of birds. Twenty-five for night-of left another six to work with.

"So, when you're living in Atlanta, will y'all come to Savannah with us in the summers?" Lynn was asking when Gennie came back outside.

"They'll want their own life, Lynn," Suzanne said. "They'll be welcome to visit whenever they want, though."

"We haven't decided that this is what we want to do," Ari said, taking the birds from Gennie.

"Why the heavens not?" Lynn asked. "Get away from that big city crowd, spend more time with real food and folk who appreciate real food."

"Atlanta *is* a big city," Gennie said. Lynn shrugged.

"Southerners appreciate food more, is all."

"Ari's family is in New York," Gennie said, gathering the

spices that Ari used for the stuffing.

"Your family doing okay in New York?" Suzanne asked Ari. "New to the country and all."

"They've done okay," Ari said.

"Momma," Gennie said.

"What?" her mother answered.

"His momma is a university professor and his daddy owns an architecture firm. They're very successful," Gennie said.

"Then they've got money," Lynn said. Gennie widened her eyes at her. Lynn ignored her, addressing Ari. "Then why are y'all in tiny little apartments?"

"Because that's what we can afford," Ari said, whisking the dry ingredients into the wet. Gennie glared at Lynn, who apparently swallowed her next question.

"It is a shame that housing in New York is so expensive," Suzanne said.

"Momma," Gennie said, feeling beset. Ari laughed.

"We like to call it cozy," he said. "We don't spend a lot of time there, anyway."

"There's stuff to *do* in New York," Gennie said. "We go places. We see things. We walk. We talk."

"There's stuff to do here," Lynn said.

"Gennie, can you get the mango prepped?" Ari asked. Gennie pulled the fruit out of the miniature outdoor refrigerator, cored it with vigor, and began chopping it, glancing up once at Lynn. Her sister shrugged.

"So who is the most interesting person you've met in New York?" Lynn asked Ari.

"We were doing a demo at a restaurant once in school, and a couple of Mets showed up, so I have a picture of that, but they weren't the most interesting. The most interesting person I know in New York is an old man who runs a fish stall at the market. He's Cambodian, and he's traveled the world more than I could almost imagine, eating at tiny little restaurants and food stands in cities all over the world. He has all of these stories that people have told him about food and politics and people. I wish I had written down everything he's told me over the last three or four years."

"People like that should write a book," Suzanne said. "Gennie's grand-daddy was like that, always talkin' about people he had met in the war and all."

Ari nodded enthusiastically, handing Gennie the mixing bowl for the sauce with a pair of oranges in it. The oranges were tricky. Mango had a pulpy, meaty flesh that cubed, crushed, and pasted extraordinarily well, but oranges were largely water and didn't naturally mix with the mango. The mango may not have had any oil in it, but the two fruits acted like oil and water. The honey was the trick to getting them to mix, though Gennie wasn't entirely sure which parts of the citrus belonged in the mix. She could squeeze the oranges and just use the juice, or she could skin them and blend them to get something the mixture of unstrained orange juice to mix in with the mango paste that her cubes would eventually become. There was a third option involving the peel itself, but she didn't actually consider the orange peel to be an edible part of the orange, so although Ari had tried several different methods so far that morning with and without the peel, it didn't make her list of options.

"How do you want to do these this time?" she asked when Ari took a breath.

"Would you mind taking a shot at them?" Ari asked. "I feel like I've tried everything and I'm looking for new ideas."

Gennie was stunned. He hadn't asked her to actually create a dish... ever, that she could think of.

"What balance do you want between the orange and the mango?" she asked. He shook his head at her, pulling up a stool and sitting, leaning on the counter.

"I want you to pick. You've got a fantastic palate, and orange and mango was your idea. I want to see how you would execute it."

She started to argue – he had done orange and mango before, after all – before realizing that he had done banana and mango, and blueberry and orange, and any of a dozen combinations involving either fruit, but he had indeed not done orange and mango together before. He watched her as though he could see her thoughts evolving.

"It's brilliant, but it's going to be hard to get right. How would you do it?"

Gennie shook her head. This wasn't her job. He cooked, she followed. Lynn seemed to sense the indecision.

"What's the big deal?" her sister asked. "You cook all day every day."

Gennie pressed her lips. Ari handed her the honey, his face not giving anything away. She searched his eyes frantically. Was this a test? Had he really run out of ideas? Was he just messing with her? She banished the final thought, trying not to look at her mother and sister.

"You went to cookin school, darlin," Suzanne said. "You know what you're doing."

Gennie grunted.

"Why is this so important to you?"

"Just take a second," Ari started, but Suzanne didn't hear that he was about to speak.

"Well, it wouldn't be, but your daddy and I paid for you to go to cooking school. Isn't this what you wanted to do?"

Of course it was. Gennie gritted her teeth. She had just never been able to – not like Ari could. She looked at the bits of mango on her fingers, frustrated.

"If you just let yourself, you can feel what is going to work right," Ari said. She looked at him and sighed, rolling her head back.

"Just tell me what you want..." she said.

"So you only work off of recipes," Lynn said. "I told you I could do that."

Gennie closed her eyes, smashing bits of fruit between her thumb and fingers.

"Honey, I thought this was what you wanted to do," Suzanne said.

"You can do this," Ari told her. Her eyes flew open.

"No. I can't, I won't, I don't want to. If you can't figure it out, do something else," she said, slamming the bowl onto the counter in front of him and turning to go into the house. She heard him sigh and Lynn make a bewildered noise before she closed the sliding door behind her.

Standing over the sink in the kitchen, the tears came. Frustrated, tired, overwhelmed, ashamed tears that she had eaten for years, believing that working with the best chef in the country could substitute for her own accomplishments. She looked at the sliding door behind her. Closed. She walked into the den, over to the window that looked out at the patio, trying to stay out of sight as she brushed still-running tears away. She could see Ari from behind as he was beating an orange against a cutting board, pre-bruising it to get juice and loose pulp out of it and getting the acidic fruit to caramelize just the slightest bit before he added it to the mango. It might work.

He will come a tiny voice in her mind said. It surprised her. She didn't want him to see her; she didn't want him to abandon what he was doing to have to come check on her. She wanted him to get it right and for everything to be right. *He will come* the voice said again. With a new wave of tears, she realized how badly she wanted him to be searching the windows of the house, rather than talking sociably with her mother and sister. He took out a mallet and started to beat the orange tentatively with it. Wasn't that going a bit far? *He will come*, the voice said again, but that might have been a question mark at the end. Gennie sniffed, biting her fingers.

"Come on..." she whispered. He hadn't even looked up. "Please..."

She waited maybe fifteen more seconds, then dropped her eyes. Sighed hard and shuddered, trying to pull herself together. She wiped harder at the tears, looking around the book shelf for a box of tissue. *He didn't come...*

She knelt to find the Kleenex on the floor-level shelf and blew her nose, trying to remind herself to breathe. 'Grow up grow up grow up grow up' she muttered under her breath, then choking on a new sob as she mentally took a step back to look at herself.

Hiding on the floor of the den at the Savannah house, hoping no one saw her, but desperately lonely. She rubbed at her eyes and blew her nose again, her throat tight and her breathing still coming in little gasps as she attempted not to sob out loud. Years of shame rained down on her as she hugged her knees and rocked on her toes. What was wrong with her?

She took three deep breaths, breathing out hard on each one to try to steady herself, then stood, her eyes closed.

When she looked up again, Ari wasn't on the back porch any more, and Lynn and Suzanne were chatting to each other. His hand was on the glass by her head, the nails neat and well-trimmed and so *Asian*. She stared at them, biting her lip. She knew those hands so well.

"Are you okay?" he asked her. She shrugged, blowing her nose again.

"None of this has been like you," he said. "Are you just stressed, or are you tired of all of this?"

"Tired of what?" she asked.

"Cooking," he said. "Performing. What we do."

She opened her mouth to deny it out of hand, then stopped. There was something there. He pounced.

"Is that what this is?"

She looked at his fingers, chewing harder on her lip.

"Gennie," he said softly, "if this isn't what you want to do, you can do something else. I can do something else. We can move to Kansas and be farmers. I could go get an architecture degree and work for my dad. I don't care. I don't want you to be unhappy."

"Momma thinks that we came here to get engaged," Gennie said. It occurred to her and was out of her mouth before she had a chance to think about whether or not she wanted to tell him that.

"Is that what you want?" Ari asked. They hadn't even started talking about getting married. Gennie looked out the window at her little sister, who was slowly transitioning from Southern belle to Southern matriarch, and Gennie knew that there would be people even here on the island who were whispering that if she didn't get it together and find herself a man, she would never have a family of which to *be* matriarch. She thought of her friends in New York, who had been living together for years and who swore that they wouldn't get married before thirty.

"No," she whispered to Ari.

"At all?" he asked, giving away a modest amount of alarm.

"Not now," Gennie said, her pulse picking up for a moment at what a miscommunication on that point had the potential to do. Ari put his arm around her waist, his chest just brushing her back.

"Are we okay?"

She dropped her head back against his chest, aware of just the smell of him, the Asian spices that his skin even now smelled of, the distinctive musk brought out by being out in the early afternoon heat and humidity, the sweet smell of mango on his breath.

"You love me more than cooking?" she asked.

"Of course," he said, his arm tightening. She paused.

"I didn't know..."

He squeezed her hard, now, bringing his other arm around her shoulders and holding her tight against his chest.

"How could you not?"

She pondered for a minute. A piece of her broke loose and she swiveled her way out of his arms.

"No." She paused. "No, no, no." She shook her head, staring down at the floor as she listened to herself for the first time since they had touched down in Atlanta. "No, no, no, no, no," she said, swinging her head back and forth now without seeing, not turning to face him, just venting. She tipped her head back at the ceiling. "No!"

She spun.

"No. You don't get to quit cooking. Stop worrying about me. I'm happy, Ari. I love you. You love me. We both know that."

She paced, circling him. He stood still, tracking her with

his head.

"It's this *place*. Ohmi*gosh* I don't want to fit in here. I sound like them, Ari. I *sound* like them. I think like them. I *eat* like them. You're right. I love it here. They just make. Me. Crazy."

She lectured the air, hands and fingers cutting through it with near-audible speed. She turned to face him, shaking her head.

"Get your show. We both know it's perfect. Let me worry about me. When I finally figure out what in the *world* I actually want to do, we'll do it."

"You don't want to cook with me?" he asked.

"Of course I do," she said, tipping her head back. Her voice grew louder. She yelled. "Of course I do."

She flipped her hands and shook her head.

"I want to cook with you and I want to eat with you and I want to shop with you. And I want to move to Atlanta and I want them all to know how amazing you are. And I want them to know how amazing your food is. I want to open a restaurant to sell it to them. I want every person in Atlanta – in Georgia – to be linin' up to…"

She paused. His stunned expression slowly altered, first to quizzical, then amusement.

"You want to open a restaurant?"

She put her hands in front of her mouth.

"I don't know. No. Yes." Her eyes wandered the floor, listening to herself. "Yes. I want to open a restaurant. I'd call it *Ari's*. I'd have a menu of all of the best foods you made on television. It would be amazing." She looked at him. "It would be amazing."

He grinned, nodding with her.

"It would. But… Gennie, you can make them better. You have no idea…"

Suddenly he swept her up, twirling her around the den. She laughed. He set her back down and took a step back, shaking his head. She waited.

"No…" he said. She waited, certain reality was going to get

her. "No," he said again. "You should call it *The Savannah House*."

She paused, then her hands flew up in front of her mouth involuntarily and she laughed. She threw her arms around his neck, then froze. Dumbfounded, she realized that she knew the best way to combine orange and mango for a sauce to go over stuffed quail.

"Ari, I need liquid nitrogen…"

ABOUT THE AUTHOR

Jamie O'Connor is one of the many identities of Chloe Garner, a wanderer with a host of identities in her head fighting each other to get out. Jamie writes stories about normal life for characters who sparkle in their own way. Find her at blenderfiction.wordpress.com on Twitter as BlenderFiction, or on Goodreads and Facebook as Chloe Garner.